CELESTE
and Crabapple Sam

by JENNIFER BRUTSCHY / illustrated by EILEEN CHRISTELOW

LODESTAR BOOKS

Dutton   New York

Library of Congress Cataloging-in-Publication Data

Brutschy, Jennifer
    Celeste and Crabapple Sam / by Jennifer Brutschy;
Illustrated by Eileen Christelow.
        p. cm.
        Summary: Bad-tempered Crabapple Sam lives alone
at the seashore, until Celeste arrives to soften him up
and renew the damaged friendship between him and
her grandfather.
    ISBN 0-525-67416-0
    [Friendship—Fiction. 2. Seashore—Fiction.]
I. Christelow, Eileen, ill. II. Title.
PZ7. B8288Ce 1994
[E]—dc20   92-1587
                                              CIP
                                               AC

Published in the United States by Lodestar Books,
        an affiliate of Dutton Children's Books.
        a division of Penguin Books USA Inc.,
    375 Hudson Street, New York, New York 10014

        Published simultaneously in Canada
        by McClelland & Stewart, Toronto

            Editor: Rosemary Brosnan
            Designer: Marilyn Granald

            Printed in Hong Kong
    First Edition 10 9 8 7 6 5 4 3 2 1

to Grandpa—never a Crabapple,
always a special friend
J. B.

Crabapple Sam was a rickety old man. He lived in a run-down bungalow way up on a cliff by the sea. He shared the house with his fat pig, Poppy, his skinny dog, Zack, and a boa constrictor named Rattlesnake.

Crabapple Sam was a sour old man, and he hid in his house like a clam in a shell. But, just to make sure that no one came calling, he put up a sign that said: BEWARE OF RATTLESNAKE.

One blustery summer day, a family moved into the beach house down the winding road. Crabapple Sam could hear children laughing and a baby crying. He covered his ears and grumbled to himself, but it didn't help at all.

That afternoon, a little girl came blowing up to his front door. He could see her through his dusty window. Her hair was tangled, and her dress was whipping around her bony knees.

When Zack saw her coming, he almost wagged his back end off. "I'm glad to meet you, too," Celeste said, rubbing his stubby fur.

"Does anybody live here?" she called out. When she got no answer, she shouted, "Can I play with your dog?"

"No!" bellowed Crabapple Sam through a broken window, and he yanked down the shade with a thump. Then he leaned back in his rocking chair and blew smoke rings around his head with an old corncob pipe.

"Don't worry. I'll see you tomorrow," Celeste whispered to Zack. She hugged him around the neck and ran down to the beach.

The next morning, Crabapple Sam ate a quiet breakfast of oatmeal and cinnamon while Zack leaned against his knee and gave a lonely whimper. Just as Crabapple Sam was slurping the last bit of milk out of his bowl, a loud *rap, trap, trap* made him spill all the milk down his chin. Zack wagged his tail and raced to the door, but old Crabapple sputtered and shouted out, "Go away, whoever you are."

"Celeste is whoever I am, and there aren't any rattlesnakes here by the sea."

"There are if I say so," Crabapple replied, throwing open the door.

"Then you aren't as smart as my Grandpa Hammond. He says they don't live around here," Celeste said.

"Did you say Hammond?" Crabapple Sam asked. He studied Celeste as though she were a puzzle. "Hmmm . . . red hair, know-it-all . . ." he mused. "You Arthur Hammond's grandkid?"

Celeste nodded and rubbed Zack's belly.

"Well," Crabapple said, waving his pipe, "you tell that old Bat Face he's wrong. One hundred percent wrong. As usual."

Celeste leapfrogged off the bungalow steps and ran down the path.

"And tell him that just because we're neighbors doesn't mean we're friends again," Crabapple Sam called out. But Celeste was already gone.

Bright and early Tuesday morning, just as Crabapple Sam popped his head out the door to check the sky and feed Poppy, Celeste came skipping up the road. "Hurumph," grumbled Crabapple, but it was too late to go into hiding.

"Why don't you pick on someone your own age?" he growled.

"Zack's nicer than my brothers, and your pig's much cuter," Celeste answered. "What's its name?"

"Her name is none of your business," said Crabapple Sam.

Celeste unlatched the gate to the pigpen at the side of the
house. "Grandpa said you're a croaky old frog. Are you?" she
asked.

Crabapple sputtered, and Celeste pulled some corn out of
her pocket. "Here, Fatso pig," she said, slipping through the
gate before Crabapple Sam could say a word.

"Her name is Poppy," Crabapple Sam said gruffly.

Crabapple Sam retreated into the house. Then he opened the window and poked his head out. "You tell that grandpa of yours that Crabapple Sam's been mad for twenty years, and he can be mad for twenty more." He pulled his head back inside, muttering, "Croaky old frog, indeed."

Celeste fed Poppy and stroked her broad back. "Good Poppy," Crabapple Sam heard her coo as she sat in the dust to feed the lumpy pig her breakfast. "Don't worry, Zack," she murmured. "I didn't forget you."

Crabapple could have closed the window, but he pretended to himself that it was stuck, and he settled into his old rocking chair. But he didn't feel like rocking, and he didn't feel like smoking his corncob pipe. He just felt like sitting and listening to Celeste's gentle whispers and Poppy's happy grunts.

Late on Wednesday afternoon, as the tide was going out, Crabapple Sam climbed down the cliff like a crab to the tide pools below. Zack ran ahead, chasing through the waves and barking at the gulls.

In front of Crabapple Sam stretched a lonely, foggy beach full of cavernous tide pools and colonies of mussels clinging to the rocks. Behind him came a call: "Wait for me!" Crabapple groaned, but he waited. Celeste picked her way across the slimy green seaweed and the slippery sandstone.

"We're having a fish fry tomorrow," she said as she caught up with Crabapple Sam, her red hair stringy and tangled. "It's at seven o'clock. Can you come?"

"Who wants to know?" asked Crabapple Sam.

"Me," said Celeste. "And Grandpa, too."

"No," answered Crabapple Sam as he set his boots to moving down the beach.

Celeste fended off Zack's sloppy tongue. "What'd you fight about, anyway?" she asked. "Grandpa wouldn't say."

Crabapple adjusted his hat. "Don't remember," he said briskly, picking his way across the rocks.

"Where are you going in those funny old clothes with that dirty old sack?" Celeste asked.

"Collecting mussels," Crabapple said. He stepped neatly around a tide pool. "Don't you ever stop asking pesky questions?"

"Can I come?" Celeste asked.

"No," said Crabapple Sam, but he didn't object when she followed him across the lonely beach.

After walking without talking for a few minutes, Crabapple Sam ventured out closer to the sea and crunched his way across the black mussels. He picked the biggest and the best and pried them off the rocks with his screwdriver.

"Why do you want mussels?" Celeste asked.

"Dinner for me and bait for rainbow perch," Crabapple Sam said, putting the mussels into his brown canvas sack.

"I have lots of muscles," Celeste said. Crabapple looked up. Celeste flexed her arm, pointed to her muscles, and laughed. Crabapple smirked and turned his back so Celeste wouldn't see him smiling.

"Can I hold the bag?" Celeste asked. He nodded and handed her the canvas sack. "It'll get heavy pretty soon," he said.

"That's okay," she answered.

"I know. You've got muscles," Crabapple Sam said. And this time he smiled at her.

All through that damp afternoon, they took turns gathering mussels. After awhile, Crabapple Sam carried the bag. "I have muscles, too," he said. But he bent lower and lower as the bag got heavier and heavier. They worked without talking until the sun was a fuzzy orange spot sinking into the ocean.

"Time to go home," Crabapple Sam said finally when the bag was filled to the brim, his back was aching, and his boots were soaked.

"I haven't seen any rattlesnakes yet," Celeste called out as they picked their way carefully across the slippery, wet rocks.

"Just you wait," said Crabapple Sam.

The bungalow was dark when they returned. Celeste stepped into the creaky little cabin, and Crabapple turned on a light.

"There's your Rattlesnake," he said, pointing to the boa, who was wrapping his powerful body around a piece of driftwood.

"Wow," said Celeste. "Is he poisonous?"

"Nope," said Crabapple. "He's just an old boa constrictor and his name is Rattlesnake."

"Pretty funny," Celeste said, and laughed. "Not as funny as me, though." She pointed to her muscles and grinned.

Crabapple dumped the mussels into a row of buckets by the door and hung his tattered hat on a rusty nail. He pulled off his water-filled boots and emptied them into the kitchen sink.

"You're invited tomorrow for rainbow perch," he said to Celeste.

"I can't," said Celeste. "Tomorrow's the fish fry. We're having halibut and watermelon and corn on the cob and s'mores."

"There's nothing like fresh perch," Crabapple Sam said, but Celeste was busy scratching Zack and didn't hear a word.

That night, while Crabapple tossed and turned in bed, he
thought about all the rainbow perch he would catch the next
day. "Enough for a good, long feast," he said. But the only
answer he got was a loud snore from Zack.

"Who needs a pesky kid and a smart-alecky old man,
anyway?" he muttered into the darkness. But it was a long
time before he was snoring, too.

The next night, at precisely seven o'clock, a sandy old man came marching up the winding road. A skinny dog was running ahead of him, a fat pig was waddling behind, and he had a boa constrictor wrapped around his neck.

"Well, I'll be jiggered," Grandpa Hammond boomed. "Here comes the biggest frog in the puddle."

"Crabapple Sam!" Celeste cried out, running to meet him. Zack barked, the baby giggled, and Celeste's brothers shouted, "A snake, a snake!"

Crabapple Sam tossed his catch of rainbow perch on the picnic table and lifted his head high. "Can't let this girl eat store-bought fish, Hammond," he said. "Fry it up nicely with plenty of butter and lime."

"Aye, aye, sir," Grandpa Hammond said, grinning. "You always were a bossy old coot."

"Like someone I know," Crabapple said, winking at Celeste.

While Celeste's parents and grandpa fried the fish and roasted the corn, Celeste, her brothers, and Crabapple Sam threw a Frisbee up and down the beach. And the whole time, Rattlesnake hung around his neck.

"How come he doesn't fall off?" one of Celeste's brothers asked.

Crabapple Sam nudged Celeste, and they shouted together, "Because he's got muscles!"

Celeste grinned, but Crabapple Sam fell down on the sand, laughing. A loud, wheezy, raspy, old laugh. And no one, not even Grandpa Hammond, was as surprised as he was.

"Croaky old frog," Celeste said affectionately. She threw herself down on the beach beside him. And the two friends rested in the sand while the fish cooked, the sun set, and Zack chased the waves off the shore.